The Pet Itch

Written by **Elli Woollard**

Illustrated by **Elina Ellis**

What Mossy the Monster most wanted to get

in the whole wide world was a small pesty pet.

A pet like an Itch with a horrible howl,

that would grizzle and grumble and guzzle and growl.

"Pets," said his granny, "are terrible creatures."

"Pets," said his uncle, "are only for teachers."

"Pets," said his aunty, "are nasty and smelly."

"Pets," said his sister, "will wee on the telly."

"All that you need," said his aunt, "are soft toys.
They won't make a **stink** or a **mess** or a **noise**."

"NO!" Mossy shouted. "They're rubbish and boring, and no good at CLAWING or GNAWING or ROARING."

"Toys," said his granny, "are cute and appealing."
"Toys," said his sister, "are brilliant for stealing."

"Pets," said his granny "are perfectly great

when you're older and bigger – you just have to wait.

... Just a few years; it won't be forever."

But would this fool Mossy the Monster? *NEVER!*

"Why," Mossy yelled, "can't I get one right *NOW?*"

("Ha!" cried his sister. "You smell like a cow!")

"Maybe," his aunt said, "you'd like to pretend
that you had a small pet; such an excellent friend!
Imaginary pets are incredibly clever."
But would this fool Mossy the Monster? NEVER!

"No!" Mossy cried. "That sounds no fun at all."

("Ha!" yelled his sister, "you're still far too small.")

"Hey!" said his uncle. "Let's go to the zoo,
and see all the animals – that's what we'll do!
Come, we'll go now, or tomorrow – whenever."
But would this fool Mossy the Monster? NEVER!

"Boring!" cried Mossy,
his thumbs in his ears.

"Boring!" cried Mossy,
trying to fake tears.

"Boring!" cried Mossy. "It's rubbish, the zoo."

("Ha," cried his sister, "you live in one too.")

"Mossy," his gran said, "I've bought you a book
with pictures of Itches. Come here, take a look.
Pictures are tidy; they don't make mess ever."
But would this fool Mossy the Monster? NEVER!

"I need a pet Itch!" Mossy cried. "Can't you see?"
("Ha!" cried his sister, "just leave it to me.")

"What we need," said his sister, "are ribbons and bows, and frills and gold sequins and pretty pink clothes."

"No!" Mossy said, "I don't like that one bit!"

"But wait!" said his sister. "This could be a hit."

The pair then went out, and soon, in a ditch.
They grabbed and they fished out a small pesty Itch.

"Sorry," said Mossy, "this small creature's fate
is already decided – it goes on my plate."

"Although," Mossy added, "I might just be kind
if you do as I tell you – I'm sure you won't mind."

"Yes!" cried the old folk. "We so love this pet!"

("Wait!" said his sister. "We've not finished yet.")

The Pet Itch

An original concept by author Elli Woollard

© Elli Woollard

Illustrated by Elina Ellis

Represented by Advocate Art

Published by MAVERICK ARTS PUBLISHING LTD

Studio 3A, City Business Centre, 6 Brighton Road, Horsham, West Sussex, RH13 5BB

© Maverick Arts Publishing Limited +44 (0) 1403 256941

First Edition Published July 2013

This Edition Published May 2015

A CIP catalogue record for this book is available at the British Library.

ISBN 978-1-84886-174-9

www.maverickbooks.co.uk